T5-AEV-768

ANTHONY'S ADVENTURES MAKING WAVES

Dr. Brenda Mitchell

This book may not be reproduced in whole or in part, in any form or by any means, electronic or mechanical, including photocopying, recording, or by any information storage and retrieval system now known or hereafter invented, without the written permission from the author.
©Copyright 2021 Brenda Mitchell. All Rights Reserved.

DEDICATION

I dedicate this book to the memory of Precious, a 1-year-old boy in Malawi who was born with albinism. He lived a brief but powerful life and touched my heart in a special way.

"I am so grateful for my family and friends who have supported me in this journey, especially my adult children who have given me so much joy and insight to appreciate the world through their eyes."

"Anthony, don't forget to pack your sunscreen!"
Mrs. Olivia, Anthony's mother, yelled as she rushed about packing for tomorrow's beach day.
"We have to pack everything we need tonight if we want to leave early in the morning," Mrs. Olivia said.
Anthony and Evan were far too excited about seeing the ocean to pack anything but swim shorts.   They jumped about their room talking about how they would swim through the big waves and make huge sandcastles. Neither boy gave any thought to what more they needed to pack.
Knowing the boys were too excited, Mrs. Olivia brought Anthony and his brother Evan, their duffle bags, extra sunscreen and a change of clothes.
She plopped the bags on the floor and smiled at her two sons. She loved the joy in their eyes as they jumped about excitedly flailing their arms to demonstrate how they would swim tomorrow.

"Ok guys, it's time to get some sleep. We'll need to get up early tomorrow, she said, trying to sound serious. Deep inside, however, she was as excited as the boys.
"Sure Mom," said Anthony.
"Yea, sure Mom," Anthony's younger brother Evan mumbled to his mother.
Anthony looked over all his stuff, and his thoughts focused on the beach…the waves…the sand and swimming faster than he had ever before. He was certain he could be an Olympic swimmer.
He imagined himself riding the waves then told his mom and brother "I can't wait to swim in the ocean!" We will have so much fun with Chris and Matt tomorrow!"
"Yea Mom…I can't wait," said Evan, still springing around the room
"It's bedtime guys…lights out in five minutes, said Mrs. Olivia.
Even after the lights were out. Mrs. Olivia could still hear her sons giggling and mumbling about going to the beach.

"Early the next morning,....

Matt and Chris came running from their home with their duffle bags while their mother followed along with more bags of snacks and beach towels.

With the bags and coolers safely packed away, the boys scrambled into the back seats of the SUV and buckled their seat belts.

Mrs. Olivia and Mrs. Lisa slipped into the car and Mrs. Olivia eased down the driveway and headed for the beach.

Anthony, Evan, Matt, and Chris were so excited. They talked over each other as they rode along bragging about how each one could swim better than the other.

"Anthony, I'm the fastest swimmer in my family," said Chris.

"Not faster than me!" Matt chimed in.

"My swimming teacher told me I was the best swimmer in the class!" Evan said louder than the rest.

"I got a trophy at the YMCA for swimming the best!" Anthony said proudly.

The mothers could only smile at each other.

"Hey look guys, I see the ocean!" Evan says while pointing from his window seat. There were a few minutes of silence as the boys watched the mighty blue ocean, the sprawling sand, the blue sky and white clouds. Their eyes followed along the beach watching all the different people walking, playing and laughing. Beach umbrellas of all different colors were sprinkled along the sand at the edge of the water. The waves of the ocean rolled on shore and then back out again.

Once the car was parked, the boys leaped out and headed for the sand.
They ran, jumped and giggled with excitement.
"Last one to the water is a rotten egg!" Evan yelled.

The four boys began to sprint.
Mrs. Olivia and Mrs. Lisa unpacked the car.
"Evan, you forgot your towel," Mrs. Olivia yelled.
Evan stopped in his tracks, turned toward his mom, then looked at the ocean again. He then headed back to get his towels while the other boys ran toward the ocean.

Mrs. Olivia and Mrs. Lisa set up their umbrellas and the snacks. Before the boys went off to play, Mrs. Olivia unpacked the sunscreen.

"Boys, don't forget the sunscreen so you can enjoy the water. Stay near our umbrella so that I see you. We will have lunch ready in a little while," she said.

Later Mrs. Olivia allowed them to go further out as she watched them play safely.

As the boys stepped closer and closer to the oceans edge, they felt the cool liquid flowing between their toes. They walked further into the shallows, before jumping into the water. It felt cool, wet and thrilling... just like they hoped!
The boys giggled and jumped around. They went further out into the ocean as the waves were getting bigger and bigger. They all were swimming and bracing for the next big wave then they looked around and noticed Anthony wasn't with them.

Anthony's arms felt like propellers...moving over and under as he went further into the ever-growing waves. Anthony was in a fog of excitement. He felt he was swimming faster than ever before. He never heard the lifeguard's whistle. He never heard people yelling from the shore. He never heard Matt and Chris yelling for him to come back!

He kicked his legs and moved ever faster. Then...

In the mirrored surface of the water, Anthony saw him.

Super Antney was there!

Anthony's super hero conscience, appeared to Anthony in the reflection of the big wave.

"Anthony, what are you doing man, you'd better go back to shore, it's dangerous out here and the lifeguard is blowing his whistle" Super Antney spoke calmly.

For a moment Anthony floated calmly in the water. Then he was clear on what he needed to do. Anthony caught the next wave headed to shore and swam with it. As he got closer to the beach, he could see his family and friends waving to him from shore.

Anthony swam faster. He wasn't sure why, but he knew he could swim back to safety. He focused on the shore...on his family. His arms felt stronger. He legs kicked harder and he could breathe easier.

The shore was not far he thought. He kept swimming. He could not stop his arms from moving, his leg kicked even stronger now.

He was met at the shore by his mom, brother, friends and other well-wishers at the beach. He could see the fear in his mother's eyes...he also saw it drain away as she hugged him. Evan, Matt and Chris were jumping all around him. Anthony felt good and safe.

"Mom, did you see how fast I swam back? Boy, am I glad you put me in swimming class at the Y. It was sooo cool!" Anthony said as he tried to catch his breath.

A crowd of people had gathered around him and his family. They were all amazed. Anthony demonstrated how he was swimming by using his arms and pointing to the waves in the ocean.

While Anthony was demonstrating his swimming skills, Mrs. Olivia struggled to put sunscreen on Anthony's arms, back, shoulders, face and legs.

As they walked back to the umbrella, Anthony was still explaining how he managed to swim so far out and then swim back.

Ian, a 7-year-old boy, from the tent next to theirs asked if he could play with them.

The boys looked at each other and agreed and in unison, "Sure, come on over!"

Ian happily joined them while they had snacks.

Ever vigilant, Mrs. Olivia knowing the impact of too much sun on Anthony's albinism, was busily checking her son's skin for signs of sun damage. She noticed Anthony was turning red. She applied more sunscreen.

"Ouch mom, it hurts when you touch me on my arms and back." Anthony said.

Ian looked curious when Anthony called Mrs. Olivia "Mom".

"Is that your mom?" You're white like me and she's brown" Ian said to Anthony.

"My skin is white because I have albinism but my family is brown like my mom and brother." Anthony said.

"What is albinism?" Ian asked.

"You see, I don't have as much skin color as the rest of my family." Anthony continued.

Evan knew that his brother had albinism, but he'd never seen his skin turn red like that and looked curious.

"Mom, why does Anthony need so much more sunscreen than I do this time?" Evan asked.

"We have to protect Anthony's skin so that he doesn't get a sunburn." Mom said.

"Everyone needs to use sunscreen but people with light skin tones need to be more careful especially with all this direct sunlight at the beach," Mrs. Olivia said as she continued applying the sunscreen.

"Anthony doesn't have as much melanin as you have. His skin will burn if we don't take special care to protect it," she said.

Evan and Anthony smile at each other as they held their arms next to each other noticing the difference as well as the similarity.

"What is melanin," Chris asked?

"That means he's not brown like me, right mom?" said Evan.

"Well that's sorta right, son," said Mrs. Olivia.

"Brown smown, I'm a red boy right now. "The sun did a job on me while I was playing in the ocean!" Anthony said.

All the children chuckled.

Matt, Chris, Ian, Evan and Anthony put their hands out to compare their colors. Brown. Brown. White. Brown and Red.

"Does it hurt?" asked Matt.

"Yep, Mom please hurry and put the aloe vera gel on. Evan, hand me my t-shirt." I need to cover up! Anthony replied.

"So Mom, where can we get Anthony more melanin so he doesn't get a sunburn like this again?" Evan asked.

"I wish it were that simple. We are born with melanin. People have different amounts of melanin based on the genes they get from their parents." Mrs. Olivia said.

"What??? Did you give us blue jeans when we were born and that makes us look the way we do???" said Evan.

"Hahaha, not jeans but genes! You wear blue jeans but the genes I'm talking about are the genes inherited from parents and passed on to their children. Both of you inherited G-E-N-E-S from us that make you look the way you do."

"So... if we have the same genes from the same parents why don't we look alike? Anthony asked.

"Glad you asked! Simple answer. It's just the way God wanted each of us to look!! Genes are combined in various ways to make people unique and special. All people are a beautiful array of shades from dark to light based on how much melanin each person has. Genes can make you look like one of your parents or a mixture of the two." she said.

Mrs. Olivia continued...the boys watched and listened.

"Chris, you have hazel eyes but your sister Brittany has dark brown eyes. Every person is different. We may have different eye color, hair color, or skin color. Our genes make everyone unique. Look at all the people on the beach. Do you see anyone who looks the same? Some are short, others tall, I see red hair, black hair, curly hair and straight hair."
"That's pretty cool," said Chris.
"Yeah, Anthony you are pretty special." said Matt.
The rest of the afternoon was spent running along the beach giggling, throwing the beach ball and snacking. It was a great day at the beach!

"Well boys, it's time to head home. Help me pack up to go!" said Mrs Olivia.
They all said goodbye to Ian and headed home. The trip back was much quieter than the trip to the beach. The boys were exhausted and fell asleep soon after they left the parking lot.

On the quiet ride home, Mrs. Lisa commented to Mrs. Oliva that she liked the way she explained genes and skin tones to the boys. She went on to say, I wish all children could be as accepting of differences as our boys are. They chatted until they suddenly realized that how close they were to home.

"Wake up boys, we're home!" Mrs. Olivia said.

Chris and Matt thanked Mrs. Olivia for a fun day and bumped fists with Anthony and Evan as they left the car to go home.

Anthony and Evan headed to their rooms to shower away beach sand and change clothes.
After his shower, Anthony stared in his mirror.
"Are you there Super Antney?" Anthony said quietly.
Super Antney appeared.
"So explain to me again why I have this sunburn?" Anthony asked.
"I don't know more than your mom already told you. But, I do know that YOU were brave and calm enough to get back to shore, my friend!" Super Antney answered.
"Yeah, I know! "laughed Anthony.

"But it's crazy that I'm called black, look white and my skin burns and makes me red!" said Anthony.

"I'm happy to be brave, calm and the best swimmer in the world with albinism!!" reflected Anthony.

"So Anthony, let's celebrate how unique you are!" said Super Antney. "Just think, when someone meets you, they don't forget you … because YOU ARE black, white or even red… give them something more to remember!! You're a great guy – smart, funny, and loyal. We are also quite handsome… if I must say so. Okay that's enough! You get my point!" Super Antney continued.

Mom came upstairs to tell Anthony and Evan that their supper is ready. She saw Anthony staring in the mirror.

"Are you feeling better?" she asked.

"I'm good, just thinking about everything that I learned today about genes and how I need to protect my special skin and celebrate ME since you and dad gave me these unique genes!" Anthony said.

"Hey mom, did you see how I handled that big wave in the ocean?"

"Yeah, that was really great!" Mom said.

"That's the Anthony that I know!! Maybe you will be my Olympic swimmer. I'm so glad to celebrate YOU and Evan as my sons! What a great day of fun in the sun!" Mrs Olivia said joyfully.

Anthony and Evan both hugged their mom. Anthony stared at their reflection in the mirror. Anthony smiled and winked at Super Antney in the mirror.

Super Antney smiled back.

THE END

What is Albinism?

"Albinism is a hereditary condition that results in a lack of pigmentation in the skin, hair and eyes." This inherited condition is characterized by a lack of the pigment melanin, resulting in pale skin, light hair, pale eyes and impaired vision. Both parents must carry the gene in order to pass it on, but they may not have albinism themselves. Although in Europe and North America approximately 1 in 20,000 people has albinism, the rates are higher in Africa, with about 1 in 1,400 occurrences in Tanzania. The term "Person with albinism" is preferred over "albino" as it puts the person ahead of their condition. – www. underthesamesun.com For more information on albinism, go to National Organization for Albinism and Hypopigmentation | Where people with albinism and their families can find acceptance, support and fellowship.

What are genes?
"Genes carry the information that determines your traits, which are features or characteristics that are passed on to you – or inherited – from your parents. Each cell in the human body contains about 25,000 to 35,000 genes." What Is a Gene? (for Kids) - Nemours Kidshealth

What is Melanin?
Melanin is a chemical that gives humans their color and protects them from the sun. The more melanin you have the darker your skin, the less melanin the lighter a person's skin tone.

Questions to make you think about yourself!

What makes you unique?
Do you celebrate those things?
Questions to make you think about the story!
What made Anthony happy about himself?
What confused Ian about Anthony and his family?
What happened when Ian asked Anthony about his mom?
How would you feel if asked about the way you or your family members look?
What can you do to make people feel welcome and accepted?

Made in the USA
Coppell, TX
29 June 2022

79392087R00024